Clock's Story

Jez Alborough

LONDON • VICTOR GOLLANCZ LTD • 1988

Dong
    dong
        dong . . .

The mantel clock struck eight times into the chilly morning at Featherby House.

"Make sure the clock is wound up today, dear," said Mr Featherby to his wife, as he was leaving for work. "Remember, tomorrow night is our New Year's Eve party, and we don't want him bringing in the New Year half an hour late in front of our guests, do we?"

Mrs Featherby passed him his case and umbrella. "I shall have Ruby see to it right away," she assured him.

"Goodbye dear. I'll be back at the usual time," said Mr Featherby, as he gave his wife a kiss and set off for the railway station.

The mantel clock had never been present at a New Year's party, and the thought of chiming such an important twelve o'clock in front of all the Featherbys' guests made him feel uncomfortably self-conscious.

As Ruby the maid wound him up he started listening to himself as he had never listened before. "Was that tick too slow for that tock," he wondered, "or was that tock too fast for that tick?" The more he thought of the party, the more he convinced himself that he was losing time.

"I mustn't slow down," he thought. "I must keep up."

Mrs Featherby noticed that it was two minutes to six when her husband returned home that evening. "You're late, dearest," she said, as she helped him off with his coat. "Did you miss your train?"

Mr Featherby checked the time on his watch. "I'm not late, dear, it's five-thirty," he said. "I always come home at five-thirty."

How silly the mantel clock felt when, just at that moment, he heard himself chime six times.

"Oh dear," said Mr Featherby. "Our clock seems to be running fast. I'd better telephone Mr Chubb the clockmaker right away, and Ruby must be told not to wind it up tomorrow — it might make matters worse."

By the time he had been taken to Mr Chubb's workroom the next afternoon, the mantel clock felt thoroughly bewildered. Dizzily he looked around and saw that he was surrounded by the numbers and hands of dozens of clock faces. Knowing that he was not telling the correct time made him feel even more lost and unsure of himself.

"I must find out the correct time," he said, "but who can I trust? Every clock here tells a different time."

To his left he noticed an old grandfather clock, whose hands pointed to eighteen minutes to three.

"Excuse me," he asked politely, "but *is* it eighteen minutes to three?"

"I'm afraid not," replied the grandfather clock. "At least, that is, it might be . . . You see, I stopped at this time three days ago. The only thing I know for sure," he chuckled, "is that once every day and once every night I'm exactly on time. Mr Chubb is too busy to mend me at the moment, so he hasn't bothered to wind me up. As every clock knows, if nobody winds you up, then sooner or later you're going to stop."

"Oh no," gasped the mantel clock. "Ruby didn't wind me up this morning. But I can't stop. Tonight is the party and I still haven't found the right time. I haven't got time to stop. And," he paused, "I'm scared. What will I do?"

"Nothing," said the grandfather clock, "just nothing."

"But that's such a shameful waste of time," cried the mantel clock.

"Not necessarily," said the grandfather clock. "Let me explain. If you look at my face you will see that as well as telling the time I also show the days of the month. Now, some months have more days than others, and sometimes, working out how to fit it all together became too much to think about. I started confusing my days with my hours and mixing my hours with my minutes.

"Before long I had lost all confidence in telling the time. Then one morning the maid forgot to wind me up and I stopped. In the gap that followed I learnt how to do nothing, and everything became simple. There are no days, hours and minutes, I realised, there is only now."

"When the maid wound me up and reset me the next morning, everything seemed to fit together again perfectly. Once you've learnt how to do nothing, you can make a much better job of doing something."

"But how do you do nothing?" asked the mantel clock.

"Well, you don't really *do* nothing," suggested the grandfather clock. "Nothing is what happens when you're not *doing* something."

The mantel clock was so confused that he hadn't realised how, gradually, during their conversation, his tick had been getting further from his tock. He did, however, feel a click inside and hear himself chime ten o'clock, slowly and distinctly off-key.

"What's wrong with me?" he croaked. "I've never chimed like that before."

Tick   tick
    tock   tock   tick . . .

At two minutes past . . . he stopped.

Everything inside was stillness. Closing his eyes he heard the silence, where previously he had uttered his steady tick tock. It seemed to swallow all his worries about the party; for in that moment, there *was* no party.

He opened his eyes and looked about him at all the other clocks. This time he noticed not only their hands and numbers, but their faces and cases too.

There was a rosewood bracket clock, a brass chiming skeleton clock, a bronze clock in the form of an Eastern palace and much more. On the bench were springs, cogs and screwdrivers, and a large magnifying glass. From his silence he looked. He was doing nothing.

Just then Mr Chubb hastened into the workroom. "It's time I fixed Mr Featherby's clock," he muttered to himself. "I promised I'd have it back and working in time for his New Year's party."

Opening the back of the mantel clock he peered inside with his eyeglass.

"Not much wrong with this one," he said, as he poked around with a screwdriver and a small oilcan. "I'll just give it a drop of oil."

Then Mr Chubb wound him up. The mantel clock smiled as he felt his springs tighten and his cogs slowly turn once again.

It was already nine o'clock by the time Mr Chubb returned to Featherby House with the clock.

"Couldn't find much wrong Mr Featherby," he said, as he carried it through the hall. "But I've oiled all the parts, so it should run smoothly now."

Mr Featherby breathed a sigh of relief. "My thanks to you, Mr Chubb," he said. "Do stay to hear it chime in the New Year."

By ten o'clock the first guests had begun to arrive for the party. By eleven o'clock the dining room was buzzing with excited guests, who from time to time looked over to the mantel clock to see how long there was to go before midnight. But the clock himself was far too interested in looking at all the happy faces to worry about bringing in the New Year.

"The time is now one minute to midnight," announced Mr Featherby. Suddenly the room fell silent, and all eyes turned towards the mantel clock, whose face wore a serene smile of understanding.

"Time," he thought, "is just another way of saying now."

Mr Featherby raised his glass, and the guests lifted theirs.

Tick   tock   tick   tock
    click
        whrrrrr
            dong
                dong
                    dong . . .

"HAPPY NEW YEAR EVERYBODY."